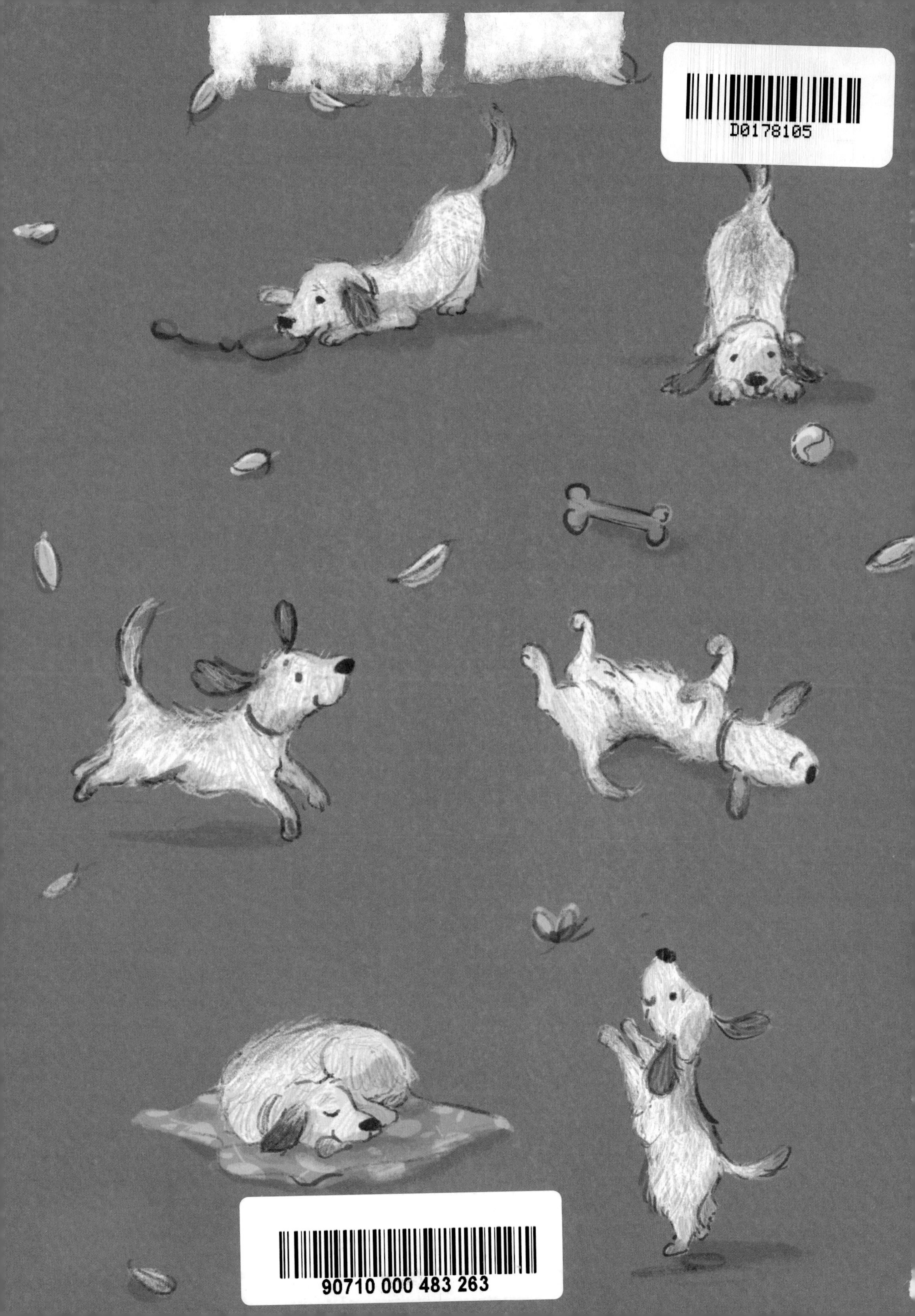

To Sara Jane — M.M.

In memory of our beloved pup, Dougal — V.B.

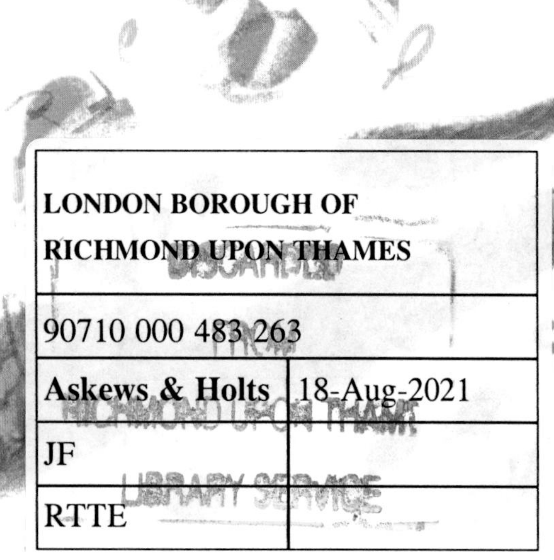

First published 2021 by Walker Books Ltd
87 Vauxhall Walk, London SE11 5HJ

This edition published 2021

10 9 8 7 6 5 4 3 2 1

This book has been typeset in Neutraface Medium

Printed in China

British Library Cataloguing in Publication Data: a catalogue record for this book is available from the British Library

ISBN 978-1-4063-8816-9 (hb) • ISBN 978-5295-0139-1 (pb)

www.walker.co.uk

Look, Puppy!

MARY MURPHY

illustrated by

VICTORIA BALL

WALKER BOOKS
AND SUBSIDIARIES
LONDON • BOSTON • SYDNEY • AUCKLAND

Hello, Puppy.

We don't know where you came from.

We don't know what kind of dog you are.

We don't even know your name.

We have been waiting

and waiting for you.

Look! Meet Mum, and Sam, and Jackie.
Meet Fairy Bell, and Teddy,
and all the crew.

You have a bowl for food,
and a bowl for water.

Here's your bed. Does it smell nice?

The apple blanket came with you.

Maybe your name

is ... Apple.

Look! The houses on our road are kind of the same and kind of different. One garden has two trees. One house is full of music.

Ayo Fashola's house is covered in roses.

Look at all the birds on his roof.

Maybe your name is Birdie, or Rose.

Look! Hands joining people together.
A skipping rope joining children together.

String joining a girl to a kite.
Maybe your name is Skippy or Kite.

There are lots more dogs down our road.
They can be your friends.

Look, meet Judy
and Honey.

Meet Ellie and Dinah,

and Dougal and Alfie.

Look! Mrs Curley
reading the newspaper,
Mr Fashola watering roses.
Push Wush the cat is going for a walk,
and so is Niamh Mooney
and her mum, Breda.
Meet Tom, Ayo,
Cormac, Sophie
and Anna.

Everyone wants to meet you,
and they all want to pick your name.
Waggy,
Momo.
Buddy-Boo,
Cutie-Pie!
Sukie,
Lodi,
Dudie,
Babe!
We don't know her name yet, I say.

Look! Birds flying,
and eating, and resting.
A squirrel busy in his own world.
Ayo training Judy,
Push Wush talking to Mr Maguire.

A pond with ducks, all different.
A frog under a leaf,
a snail looking for dinner.
Look, Puppy.

Puppy?

Puppy?

PUPPY!

Where are you?

Sukie,
Lodi,
Buddy-Boo,
Kite!

Waggy,
Dudie,
Momo,
Babe!

Apple,

Birdie,

Skippy,

Rose!

Puppy! Where are you?

I've looked and looked.
Now I want to think.

Where would I go,
if I were a puppy?

I know where you could be.

There you are, under your blanket.

This puppy needs some peace and quiet, I say.

This puppy is going home.

It seems we're all going home.
Push Wush, Mr Maguire and Niamh Mooney.
Mum, and Sam, and Jackie, and you and me.
But you don't need to look at them, Puppy.
Sometimes you want to look and look.
Sometimes you want to think.

My Puppy! You're a treasure, and a friend, and a star.

And now I know your name.

It's Apple

Birdie

Skippy

Rose

Sukie

Lodi

Buddy-Boo

Kite

Cutie-Pie

Dudie

Momo

Babe

Waggy

Star.

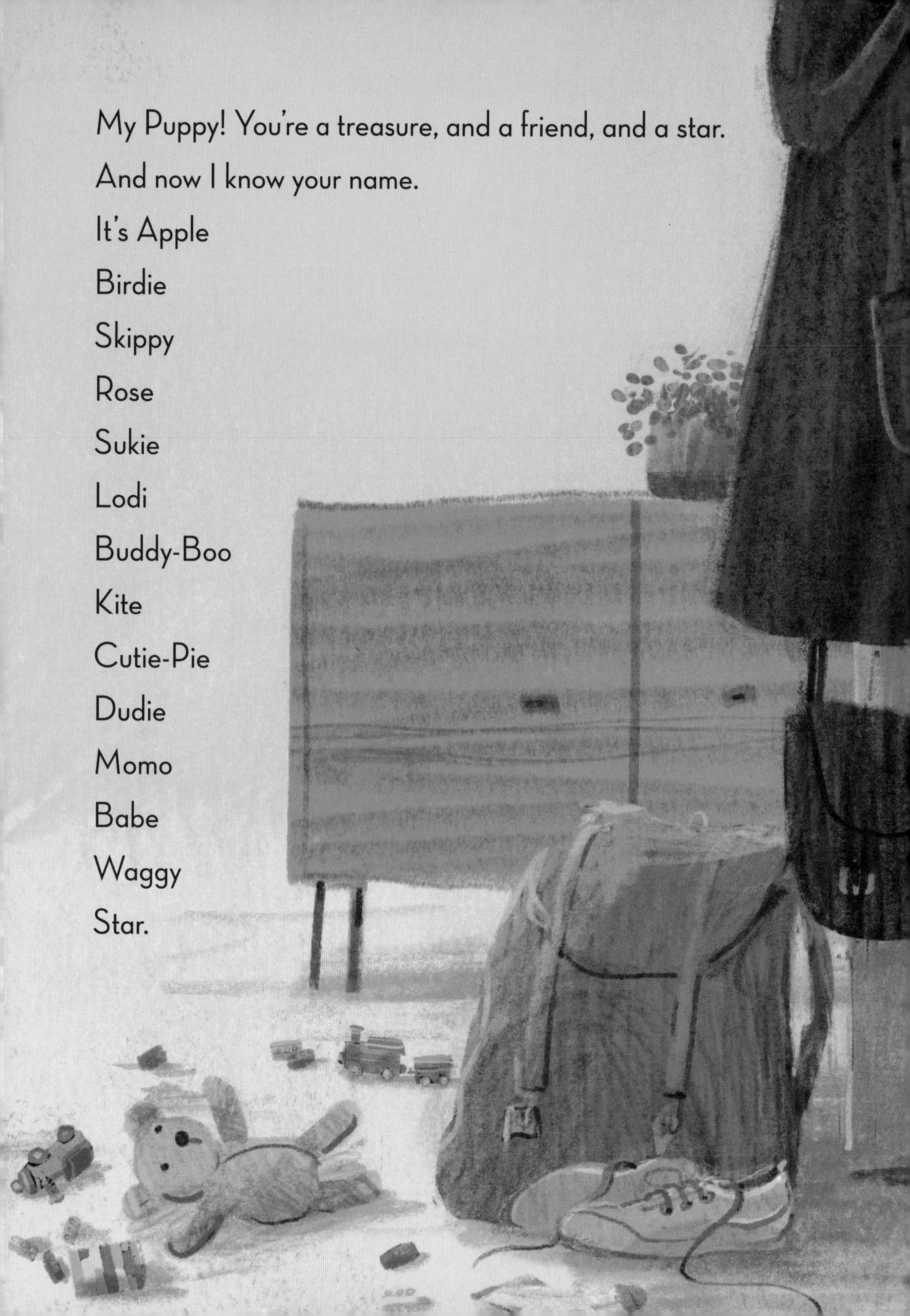

But I'll just call you Star.